Originally published in the Netherlands by
Lemniscaat b.v. Rotterdam under the title *Meisjes om te zoenen*

Printed in Belgium
First U.S. edition, 2007

CIP data is available

LEMNISCAAT
An Imprint of Boyds Mills Press, Inc.
815 Church Street
Honesdale, Pennsylvania 18431

The Sweetest Kiss

Maranke Rinck

ILLUSTRATIONS BY

Martijn van der Linden

Lemniscaat
Asheville, North Carolina

The Prince on the Palace Floor

"Hello!"

"Hey!"

"Yoo-hoo! Prince!"

Outside there's the sound of shouting.

Inside is the prince, sitting on the palace floor.

He's looking into his crystal ball. "I see girls," he whispers.

"That's right," answers the ball. "They are just outside the gates."

The prince stares and stares. "They're so beautiful!"

"Yes," says the ball, "aren't they? And they all want to kiss you."

The prince smiles shyly and fiddles with his crown. "But I'm only a frog," he says. "Don't they know that?"

"They know," says the ball. "But it doesn't matter. After all, you're a prince, aren't you? Girls love princes."

"Are you sure?" asks the prince.

"I'm sure," says the ball. "Just take your pick."

"But which one should I choose?"

"The sweetest," says the ball.

"The sweetest," sighs the prince. "That's going to be hard. There are so many."

"I'll send them in one by one," says the ball.

"All right," says the prince. He takes a deep breath. "Open the gates!" he cries.

The Hummingbird at the Gates

"Good morning, ladies," calls a voice. "Glad you could come. Take a look around the palace. The prince will meet with you one by one. After that he'll decide which one is sweetest."

The hummingbird has been sitting above the gates since dawn. *Oh boy, I'm first*, she says to herself.

She looks at the other girls, at how they're pushing and shoving. She chuckles. *One of them has floppy ears. And that hippopotamus back there—what a big nose!*

Suddenly she catches herself. She shakes her head. *Those aren't very sweet thoughts.*

And the prince is going to pick the *sweetest* girl!

"Big noses are chic," she mumbles. She's feeling a bit sweeter already. "Very chic!" she says out loud.

A couple of the girls look at her.

She nods at them and waves to the hippo, as sweet as you please.

"Miss Hummingbird," calls the voice. "You may go in first."

The gates open and the hummingbird tumbles into the hall.

"Come with me," says the crystal ball. "I'll take you to the prince."

The Hippo in the Hall

The girls disappear into the palace. "Oh!" they cry in amazement. "How beautiful!"

Only the hippo lingers behind in the empty hall. "Good luck," she calls to the hummingbird. "I'll just wait here!"

Here! the hall echoes.

"I still don't have an opening line," the hippo mutters, "for later on, when it's my turn."

Deep in thought, she walks across the tiles. "Hello, prince," she starts out. "You'd be bliss to kiss." She screws up her face. That's not it.

"Prince," she says, trying once again. "I'm all aflame. One kiss from me and you'll never be the same." She bursts out laughing.

"Prince, my pet. My kiss is something you'll never forget." She purses her lips and makes a big smack in the air.

A kiss comes echoing back through the hall.

The hippo laughs—so hard that she almost falls over. Tears run down her cheeks and fall to the floor. "It's nerves," she mutters after catching her breath. "I'll just get a drink of water from the kitchen."

The Foxes in the Kitchen

Sitting at the kitchen table are two little foxes. Startled, they look up at the door, which is slowly opening.

The hippo peeks inside.

"We haven't touched anything!" cry the foxes with their mouths full. In front of them is an empty dish.

"Calm down," says the hippo. "I just want a little water."

She walks to the tap and takes a drink. "Goodness gracious," she says. "At first I couldn't find the kitchen. I almost walked into the throne room!"

"Oh?" the foxes ask with curiosity. "And, did you see anything?"

"I wasn't allowed in," says the hippo. "The hummingbird was still wrapped up in her meeting with the prince, I suspect. See you later!" She walks out of the kitchen.

"Did she just say the hummingbird was all wrapped up with the prince?" asks one fox.

The other fox nods. "I think she did!"

They jump up. "Then all the girls should be told!" the first fox shouts.

"You go to the ballroom. I'll go to the library."

The Curlew in the Library

The curlew is standing in front of a bookcase. She's thinking about what the fox just told her: the hummingbird was all wrapped up with the prince.

"Will he still want to see me?" she sighs.

"Next!" cries a voice. "Miss Curlew!"

The curlew strikes her breast with one wing. "Oh, dear!"

Across the carpet a crystal ball rolls up to her. "Hello," says the ball. "I hope I didn't frighten you."

Unable to speak, the curlew shakes her head.

"Fine," says the ball. "I'll take you to the prince. First you'll be introduced to him. Then you'll have a little chat. Just be yourself!"

"Myself?" she asks, running after him nervously.

The ball stops once again. "Would you like a tip? I'll give you a tip."

The curlew leans close to the ball.

"Be your *sweet* self," whispers the ball, and starts rolling again. "Good. We'll go through this door. The other one goes to the ballroom. Come on!"

THE KANGAROO RAT IN THE BALLROOM

"Three's a lucky number," says the kangaroo rat.

She kisses her necklace, runs through the ballroom and jumps. "Not on a crack!" she cries before landing on the tiles.

Crestfallen, she looks down at her feet. "Oops," she says. "So much for cracks."

She looks around. No one else can be seen. The ballroom is empty. She quickly steps off the crack.

"Yes!" she cheers. "Right in the middle of the tile! If that's not good luck, I don't know what is!"

Something's tickling her cheek. She brushes it aside with her paw. "An eyelash!" she cries happily. "Now I can make a wish." She blows the eyelash away. "I wish the prince would choose me and not that stuck-up hummingbird!"

She opens a door. Another girl waits in the hall. The kangaroo rat stares at her.

"A black cat," she mutters. She shakes her head. "Oh, it's all just superstition." And with one leap she jumps up over the black cat and into the hall.

The Black Cat in the Hall

The kangaroo rat glances back at the black cat. "Listen, shorty," she whispers. "The hummingbird was snuggling on the prince's lap. So don't think *you* stand a chance." Then she jumps away.

The black cat frowns. "Shorty?"

She enters another hall with windows down to the floor. Some of them are open. It smells like a garden. "I'm not afraid to snuggle on laps," she mutters.

She pauses and looks into the palace garden. Little pathways wind along the flower beds. There's a summer house and even a fountain. Rays of sunlight tickle the black cat's fur.

"It feels like my palace already," she says. "I'm going to kiss the prince. Then he'll be very handsome. And we'll live happily ever after."

She goes to the end of the hall and walks outside. The fountain is spraying. Drops of water glisten in the sun. She grins. "Don't we have good taste, the prince and I? Our fountain is so beautiful!"

The Gannet at the Fountain

The gannet sticks her head under the stream of water and gives herself a shake. Her feathers stand straight up.

"Very becoming," says the black cat.

"Latest thing," grins the gannet. She starts combing her feathers.

The black cat takes a walk around the fountain.

"Am I short?" she asks suddenly.

The gannet looks at her. "Well ...," she says with hesitation.

The black cat wrinkles her nose.

"Short and sweet," says the gannet.

The black cat beams.

The gannet pats her hairdo carefully.

"Did you hear about the hummingbird?" asks the black cat.

"No," says the gannet.

"She was snuggling on the prince's lap," continues the black cat, "cheek to cheek."

"Really?" The gannet sniffs. "Well!"

The black cat nods.

"Will you excuse me?" says the gannet, ruffling her feathers. "My feathers are too greasy. I'm heading for the bathroom."

The Polar Bear in the Bathroom

The polar bear is standing before a mirror. She examines her head from every angle. She sticks out her tongue. She wiggles her nose.

"No," she finally decides. "I *don't* look like a frog."

Not far away the gannet is taking a bath. She almost chokes. "The prince doesn't want you to look like a frog at all," she laughs. "What he wants is a sweet girl."

The polar bear isn't so sure. "But he's the only frog here."

"Yes," says the gannet. "Until you kiss him. Then everything changes."

"Oh," says the polar bear. "That's good. Then at least I stand a chance."

The gannet blows a soap bubble at her. "By the way, I heard the hummingbird was nuzzling his cheeks."

The soap bubble explodes.

"Nuzzling?" The polar bear shrugs her shoulders. "Oh, well. The hummingbird doesn't look like a frog either."

The gannet groans. "Oooh! I give up. ..."

The polar bear smiles. She walks out of the bathroom and down the stairs.

The Hedgehog on the Stairs

The hedgehog slides down the bannister. She lowers her head and zooms around the curves.

"Hello!" she calls to the polar bear.

The polar bear stops on one of the steps. "What are you doing?" she asks with surprise.

"I'm sliding," cries the hedgehog. "It's wonderful!"

"Is that allowed?" asks the polar bear. "I'd watch out if I were you."

The hedgehog keeps on sliding.

"Hey," the polar bear shouts after her. "Did you hear about the hummingbird?"

"Yes," the hedgehog shouts back. "But I pay no attention to gossip!"

"And did you know she's already been nuzzling with the prince?"

The hedgehog speeds up. "All that fuss and tittle-tattle," she mumbles. "Just a lot of girl stuff."

She gets to the bottom and jumps from the bannister. "There," she says. "I don't care what the prince looks like after the kiss." She trembles a bit. "As long as he doesn't turn into a girl!"

The Rabbit in the Throne Hall

The rabbit is looking for a place among the other girls.

Her heart is pounding.

This is it.

Before them stands the prince. "Dear girls," he begins. "I am now going to tell you who I think is the sweetest."

He looks from girl to girl.

The rabbit blushes.

"You're going to pick the hummingbird!" shouts one of the girls.

"Yes, we knew it all along!" cries another.

The prince sighs. "The hummingbird," he says dreamily.

The rabbit bites her lip.

"No," the prince continues. "Not just the hummingbird." He takes a breath. "It may sound a bit strange, but I can't decide. ... I love you all!"

He shuts his eyes. "Whoever loves me, too, may come and kiss me."

"I love you!" cries the rabbit. She runs up to the prince.

And she's not the only one.

All the other girls race toward him. And kiss him. And then it happens ... the big change!

The prince's crystal ball cheers.

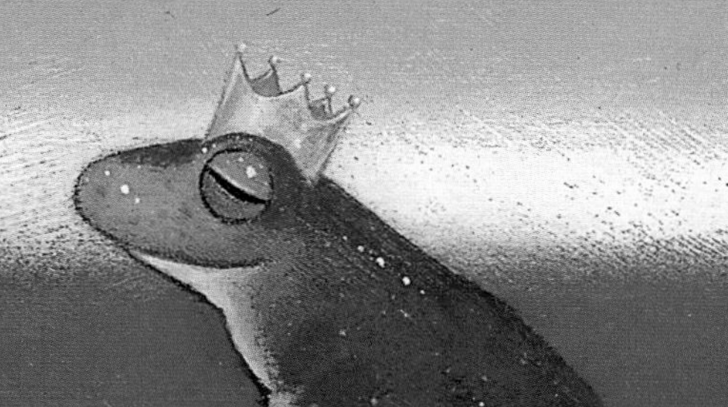

The Prince and the Princesses on the Palace Floor

The girls point to each other.

"Oooh, you should see yourself!"

"And you! You, too!"

They start jumping across the room in astonishment.

The prince is still sitting on the palace floor. He looks at his princesses with beaming eyes.

One princess with a pointed nose jumps next to him.

A black princess follows her. She presses her head against his shoulder. "How handsome you are," she says softly.

All the princesses wrap themselves around him.

Even his crystal ball rolls nearer. "So?" asks the ball. "Was it worth the wait?"

"Yes!" cries the prince. He puts his arms around his princesses. "This is more than I ever dared to dream."